For the Tigers -
Noah, Will, Tim and Antonia
~JS and TW

LITTLE TIGER PRESS
An imprint of Magi Publications
1 The Coda Centre, 189 Munster Road
London SW6 6AW
This paperback edition published in 2001
First published in Great Britain 2001
Text © 2001 Julie Sykes
Illustrations © 2001 Tim Warnes
Julie Sykes and Tim Warnes have asserted their rights
to be identified as the author and illustrator of this work
under the Copyright, Designs and Patents Act, 1988.
Printed in Belgium by Proost NV, Turnhout
All rights reserved • ISBN 1 85430 723 1
3 5 7 9 10 8 6 4 2

Wait for me, Little Tiger!

by *Julie* Sykes

illustrated by Tim Warnes

LITTLE TIGER PRESS
London

Little Tiger had lots of friends. They liked to play exciting games. Each time he went out to look for them his little sister would say, "I'm lonely. Can I come with you, Little Tiger?"

And Little Tiger would answer,
"No you can't, Little Sister. You're
much too small."

One day, Little Tiger said, "Can I go out to play?"
Mummy Tiger was very busy, so she told him to take Little
Sister along, too.
"I don't want to!" cried Little Tiger. "She's much too small
to play with me."
But Mummy Tiger wouldn't change her mind. "She's not
too small, if you lend her a paw now and then," she said.

Crossly, Little Tiger ran off into the jungle.
"Wait for me!" cried Little Sister,
scampering after him.

Little Tiger took Little Sister to visit Little Bear.
They played skittles, but Little Sister couldn't
roll the ball straight.
She missed the skittles, and hit Little Bear instead.

"Ouch!" cried Little Bear, nursing her paw. "Perhaps you should find somewhere safer to play." Little Tiger thought so, too. "Wait for me!" cried Little Sister, as he hurried towards the trees.

Very soon Little Tiger came across
Little Monkey. They both climbed
up trees and swung down vines.
But Little Sister couldn't climb
trees. She reached the first
branch, then fell and landed
on top of Little Monkey.

"Ouch!" he squeaked.
Little Tiger sighed. He didn't
want to leave his game with Little
Monkey, but it wasn't safe enough
for Little Sister. He would have to
take her away from the trees.
"Wait for me!" cried Little Sister,
bouncing after him.

Little Tiger went to find Little Leopard. His spotty friend was running in the grass. Little Leopard started a chase, but Little Sister didn't look where she was going. She tripped on a stone, hurtled forward and knocked Little Leopard flat on his face.

"Ow!" cried Little Leopard. "That hurt!"
Little Tiger was worried he would have no
friends left, if Little Sister kept causing accidents.
"Come along," he said. "We'd better go
somewhere else."

Little Tiger trotted off to the river, where he found Little Elephant on the bank. Little Sister couldn't wait to learn how to swim.

"It's easy," said Little Tiger, jumping in. "You kick your paws and off you go!"

Little Sister didn't find swimming easy. The water splashed in her eyes and she couldn't see where she was going. Suddenly . . .

and Little Sister swallowed a mouthful of water.
"Help!" she spluttered.
Little Tiger towed her safely to the bank.
"Swimming is too dangerous for you," he said.
"You'd better sit and watch."

"I don't *want* to watch. I want to play with you," she shouted crossly. "You're much too little to play my games," said Little Tiger.

Little Tiger jumped back into the water. It was fun splashing around with Little Elephant. Soon he forgot all about Little Sister on the bank. He only remembered her when the game was finished. "That was fun, wasn't it, Little Sister?" he called. There was no answer.

When Little Tiger jumped out of
the water, the riverbank was empty.
His little sister had gone!

Little Tiger felt really awful. He should not have left Little Sister on her own. What if she had fallen into the water and been swept away?

Little Elephant helped him search along the riverbank, but they couldn't see her anywhere.

Little Tiger looked everywhere.
He searched the plains,
but she wasn't there.
He hunted in the trees,
but she wasn't there.

He peered inside Little Bear's
cave, but she wasn't there either.
Now Little Tiger was frightened.
Mummy Tiger would be so angry
that he had lost Little Sister.
Sadly, he ran home to tell her.

He was almost there when . . .

"BOO!"

Little Sister leapt down
at him from the trees.

"See, Little Tiger," she cried.
"I've been practising and
now I can climb trees, too!"

Little Tiger was so pleased that Little Sister was safe.
He wanted to make it up to her for being unkind.
"I'll help you practise at skittles next," he offered.
"And running?" asked Little Sister.
"And running," Little Tiger agreed.

"Good," she said. "And after all that, will you help me to swim?"
"Maybe," said Little Tiger. "But for now, Little Sister, it's time I helped you home."

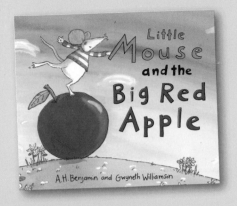

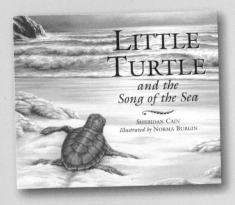

Catch up with the best from
Little Tiger Press

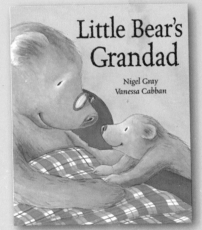

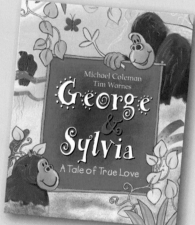

For information regarding any of the above titles
or for our catalogue, please contact us: Little Tiger Press,
1 The Coda Centre, 189 Munster Road, London SW6 6AW, UK
Telephone: **020 7385 6333** Fax: **020 7385 7333**
e-mail: info@littletiger.co.uk